PJMASKS

BE A HERO!

Based on the episode "May the Best Power Win"

Simon Spotlight
New York London Toronto Sydney New Delhi

SIMON SPOTLIGHT
An imprint of Simon & Schuster Children's Publishing Division
1230 Avenue of the Americas, New York, New York 10020
This Simon Spotlight edition December 2019
This book is based on the TV series PJ MASKS © Frog Box / Entertainment One UK Limited / Walt Disney EMEA Productions Limited 2014;
Les Pyjamasques by Romuald © (2007) Gallimard Jeunesse. All Rights Reserved. This book/publication © Entertainment One UK Limited 2019.
Adapted by May Nakamura from the series PJ Masks
SIMON SPOTLIGHT and colophon are registered trademarks of Simon & Schuster, Inc.
For information about special discounts for bulk purchases, please contact Simon & Schuster Special Sales at 1-866-506-1949 or business@simonandschuster.com.
Manufactured in the US 0620 LAK
4 6 8 10 9 7 5
ISBN 978-1-5344-5262-6
ISBN 978-1-5344-5263-3 (eBook)

Gekko, Catboy, and Owlette love being heroes! Every night they work hard to stop the villains from messing with your day. Throughout their adventures they've learned what it takes to be great heroes.
Do *you* want to be a hero like the PJ Masks?

During the day Amaya, Connor, and Greg are kids just like you. They always have their eyes and ears open to notice when something isn't quite right—like missing museum artifacts or a Sticky-Splatted library!

Once they notice something is wrong, they can do something to help fix it.

HEROES ARE CURIOUS!

Today after school the PJ Masks can't stop talking about their brand-new superpowers.

"I can't wait to go practice them tonight!" Greg says.

"Our new powers are amazing," Connor agrees.

There is a strange noise behind them, and the three friends turn around.
"What was that?" Connor asks.
"One of the villains must be up to something!" says Gekko.

HEROES PAY ATTENTION!

It's time for the PJ Masks to go into the night to save the day!

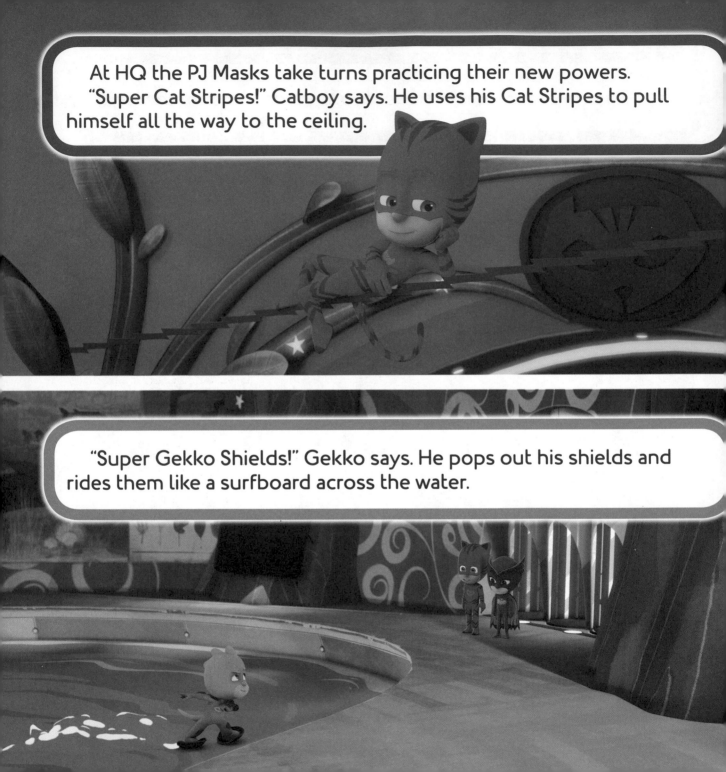

At HQ the PJ Masks take turns practicing their new powers. "Super Cat Stripes!" Catboy says. He uses his Cat Stripes to pull himself all the way to the ceiling.

"Super Gekko Shields!" Gekko says. He pops out his shields and rides them like a surfboard across the water.

"Super Owl Feathers!" says Owlette as she swoops through rings. She aims carefully, and her feathers hit a practice target perfectly. "Bull's-eye!" she shouts.

HEROES ARE PRECISE!

The PJ Masks love their powers so much that they run outside to test them in the city.

WHETHER THEY RUN FAST, FLY HIGH, OR LIFT HEAVY THINGS, HEROES ARE ON THE GO!

Outside, the PJ Masks run into Romeo and his robot. "You better watch out!" Owlette brags.

"Why? Because of your new fancy feathers, kitty stripes, and a few extra lizard scales?" Romeo says, yawning.

The PJ Masks are confused. How does Romeo already know about their new powers?

Before they can find out, Romeo's robot runs toward them.
"Super Cat Stripes!"
"Super Owl Feathers!"
"Super Gekko Shields!"
The PJ Masks quickly defeat the robot.

The PJ Masks grin as Romeo drives off in defeat. With their new powers, the heroes are feeling super proud, super strong, and . . . *super awesome*!

JUST LIKE EVERYONE ELSE,
HEROES HAVE BIG FEELINGS!

But Romeo isn't finished with the PJ Masks yet. He returns and this time his robot is wearing a new All-in-One Power Belt!

Gekko throws a shield, but Romeo's robot pushes a button on the Power Belt. It emits a vibration, making the shield wobbly and hard to control.

Romeo's robot pushes another button, and the Power Belt throws Catboy's stripes to the ground. Another button blows Owlette's feathers back at her.

This time Romeo beats the PJ Masks!

HEROES AREN'T PERFECT; THEY MAKE MISTAKES TOO.

Romeo traps the PJ Masks in a cage. He has been spying on them all day and all night. Hearing them brag about their powers has helped him come up with the All-in-One Power Belt invention.

"Now I'm free to rule the world!" Romeo yells.

Gekko, Catboy, and Owlette have been so busy showing off their powers that they have forgotten the most important part of their hero work: protecting the city.

NO MATTER WHAT THEIR MISSION MAY BE,
HEROES ALWAYS REMEMBER WHAT'S IMPORTANT!

Soon PJ Robot arrives from HQ. He tries to help break open the cage, but he can't find a way to free the PJ Masks.

"I can't believe it. Romeo's won," Owlette says.

Then PJ Robot starts talking rapidly. Owlette, Gekko, and Catboy listen closely to his instructions. If they want to escape the cage and defeat Romeo, they need to understand the whole plan.

HEROES LISTEN TO EACH OTHER!

The PJ Masks launch into their plan.

"Nothing compares to PJ Robot's secret power," Gekko calls out to Romeo.

"Hmmm. We'll see about that," Romeo replies. His robot chases after PJ Robot, who dodges and distracts the villains.

Meanwhile the PJ Masks stay focused and don't let their new powers get in the way of the mission. They work together to roll the cage forward. Just as Romeo's robot is about to hit the Power Belt's vibration button, the cage lands in front of him.

The vibration breaks the cage open. The PJ Masks are free!

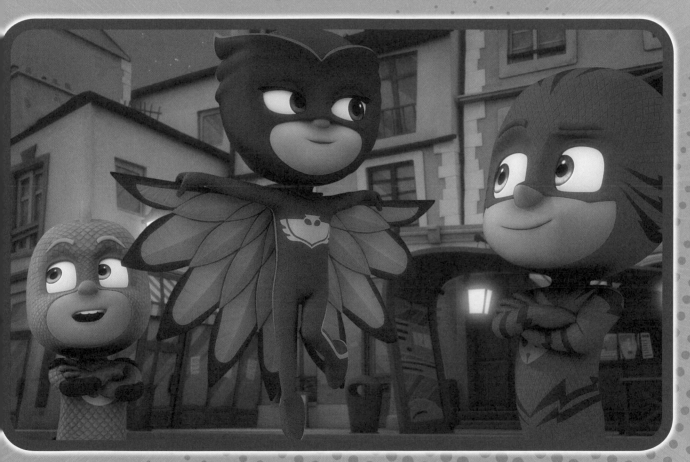

HEROES STAY CALM AND STICK TO THE PLAN.
HEROES THINK BEFORE THEY ACT!

Owlette traps Romeo with her Super Owl Feathers. Gekko deflects the robot's zaps with his Super Gekko Shields.

Meanwhile Catboy uses his Super Cat Speed to take the All-in-One Power Belt away from Romeo's robot. "We're keeping this in HQ, safe and sound," he says.

The All-in-One Power Belt might have defeated the heroes one at a time. But this time the PJ Masks have worked together to defeat Romeo. They might have lost once, but the PJ Masks don't give up.

NOT EVERYTHING WORKS ON THE FIRST TRY.
HEROES KEEP TRYING!

"I'll get you next time, PJ Masks!" Romeo shouts as he drives off. The PJ Masks smile at each other. Tonight they have used the most important power of all . . . working together the PJ way!

Gekko, Catboy, Owlette, and PJ Robot all have their own special powers. And when they work together, they can't be defeated!

HEROES ARE TEAM PLAYERS!

Everyone can be a hero . . . yes, that means you, too! Just follow in the footsteps of Owlette, Catboy, and Gekko. If you work hard and keep trying, soon you'll be unstoppable!

Are you ready to go into the night to save the day with the PJ Masks?
It's time for you to be a hero!
PJ Masks all shout hooray! 'Cause in the night, we saved the day!

BE A HERO!

HEROES ARE CURIOUS!
- Always keep your cat ears and owl eyes open. You never know when you might find a problem that needs solving or someone who needs your help.

HEROES PAY ATTENTION!
- When you focus on the task in front of you—at school or at home—you might learn something that will help your mission.

HEROES ARE PRECISE!
- Practicing your skills—whatever they may be—will make you better at them.

HEROES ARE ON THE GO!
- You don't need to be super fast or super strong to be a hero. Just be ready to spring into action when there's something that needs to be done!

HEROES HAVE BIG FEELINGS!
- If you're feeling mad or scared, take a deep breath. You'll feel more ready to save the day.

HEROES AREN'T PERFECT.
- Everyone makes mistakes, and you will too. It takes a lot of practice to master your superpowers.

HEROES ALWAYS REMEMBER WHAT'S IMPORTANT!
• Not all heroes have the same mission. What's important to you? What do you want to accomplish?

HEROES LISTEN TO EACH OTHER!
• Even though you might not agree, always listen to your fellow heroes. They might have a super idea that you haven't thought of yet.

HEROES THINK BEFORE THEY ACT!
• Be patient, make a plan, and stick to it. It will make you a stronger hero.

HEROES KEEP TRYING!
• Don't give up if your plan doesn't work right away. Sometimes it takes a few tries before you accomplish your goal.

HEROES ARE TEAM PLAYERS!
• You're stronger when you work together!

ALWAYS REMEMBER: YOU CAN BE A HERO, JUST LIKE THE PJ MASKS!